For all the children who helped me
with ideas for this book,
thank you.

SHARK IN THE DARK!
A DAVID FICKLING BOOK 978 1 849 92018 6

First published in Great Britain 2009 by David Fickling Books,
a division of Random House Children's Books
A Random House Group Company

This edition published 2010

5 7 9 10 8 6

Copyright © Nick Sharratt, 2009

The right of Nick Sharratt to be identified as the author and illustrator of this work
has been asserted in accordance with the Copyright, Designs and Patents Act 1988.

DAVID FICKLING BOOKS
31 Beaumont Street, Oxford, OX1 2NP

www.kidsatrandomhouse.co.uk

Addresses for companies within The Random House Group Limited can be found at:
www.randomhouse.co.uk/offices.htm

THE RANDOM HOUSE GROUP Limited Reg. No. 954009

A CIP catalogue record for this book is available from the British Library.

Printed in China

 Hello, Finn!

Shark in the Dark!

Nick Sharratt

David Fickling Books

Just before bedtime,
a certain small boy
stands at the window
with his favourite toy.

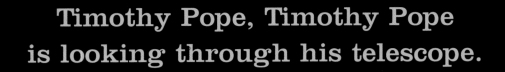

Timothy Pope, Timothy Pope
is looking through his telescope.

He looks at the sky
and the moon up there.

He looks left.

He looks right.

He looks
everywhere.

And this
is what he sees.

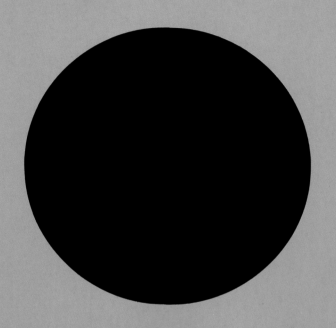

Jumping jellyfish!
What's that bobbing in the dark?
Could it be a
GREAT
WHITE
SHARK?

A shark?
No it's not.
It's the sail on
a yacht!

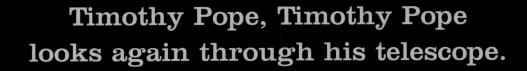

Timothy Pope, Timothy Pope
looks again through his telescope.

He looks at the sky
and the moon up there.

He looks left.

He looks right.

He looks
everywhere.

And this
is what he sees.

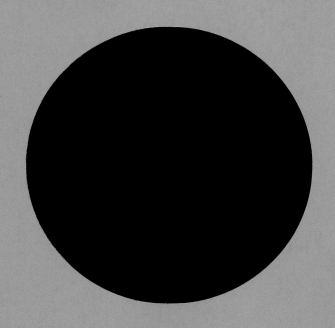

Stumbling starfish!

What's that swishing through the dark?
Could it be a

GREAT
WHITE
SHARK?

Tim says, "Silly me!

It's a seagull with his tea!

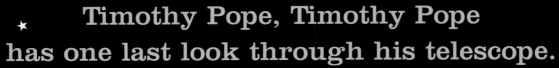

Timothy Pope, Timothy Pope
has one last look through his telescope.

He looks at the sky
and the moon up there.

He looks left.

He looks right.

He looks
everywhere.

And this
is what he sees.

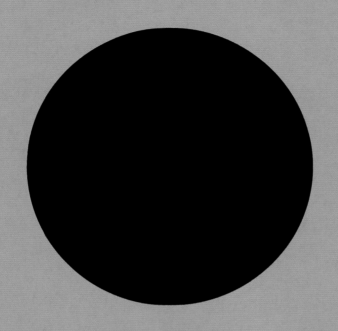

Quivering catfish!

What's that lurking in the dark?
Could it be a

GREAT
WHITE
SHARK?

Don't worry Tim,
there's no need to scream.

It isn't a shark,
it's a giant
ice cream!

Tim says to his dad,
"I'm sure I'm right.
There are no sharks
in the dark tonight."